DENNY DAVIDSON, DETECTIVE

Written by
Susan Griffiths

Illustrated by
Trish Hill

HORWITZ
MARTIN
EDUCATION

Contents

Chapter 1

Denny Davidson, Detective

My name is Denny Davidson. I'd like to be a detective when I grow up. My job will be to follow people and find out what they do.

Even though I'm only eight years old, I've already started pretending to be a detective.

Sometimes, even the best detectives get into trouble, though. I'm in trouble now! People don't believe my story—but I'll tell you about a detective job I did yesterday. You can make up your own mind!

I was following Mickey and Maude, the Macintosh twins. We were on a school trip at the museum, and I knew that they were up to no good. They're lazy. I was going to follow them and get them into trouble.

While the rest of our class was in another room of the museum, Mickey and Maude sneaked into a room full of old jars.

They sat down and started to yawn. Like a good detective, I hid behind the door, and wrote down what I saw.

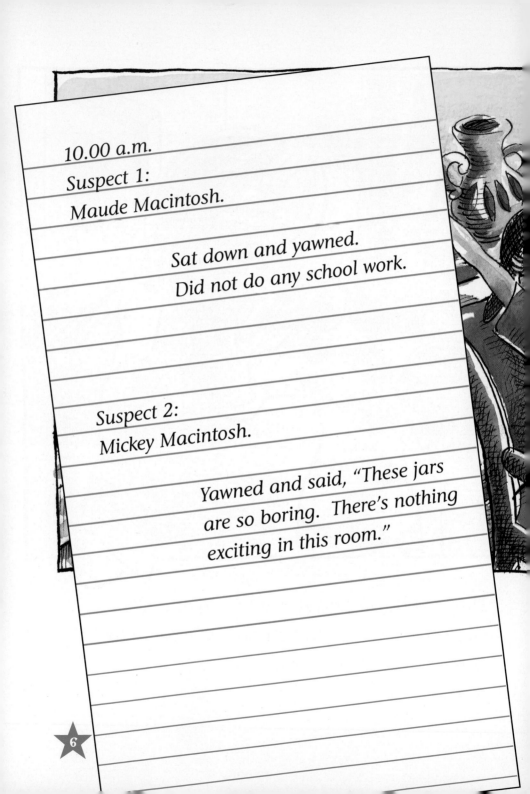

10.00 a.m.

Suspect 1:

Maude Macintosh.

Sat down and yawned.
Did not do any school work.

Suspect 2:

Mickey Macintosh.

Yawned and said, "These jars
are so boring. There's nothing
exciting in this room."

This was great. They were being lazy. I was really going to get those twins into trouble when I told our teacher, Mrs Hartley.

Chapter **2**

An Accident

There I was, hiding behind the door, breathing silently. Then, I couldn't believe my luck! Mickey did something really bad. He broke one of the museum's jars!

I was sure he would say it was an accident, so I wrote down what happened.

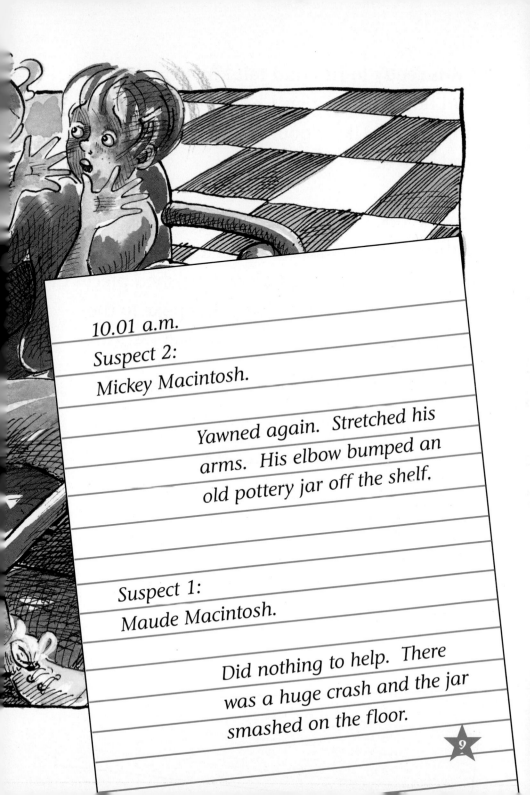

10.01 a.m.

Suspect 2:

Mickey Macintosh.

Yawned again. Stretched his arms. His elbow bumped an old pottery jar off the shelf.

Suspect 1:

Maude Macintosh.

Did nothing to help. There was a huge crash and the jar smashed on the floor.

I was ready to run and tell Mrs Hartley what
had happened, when something really strange
happened. Like a good detective, I had to stay
and watch.

On the floor, where the jar had broken,
a strange-looking person uncurled himself.
He blinked and squinted and brushed pieces of
pottery off his clothes. Then, he spoke to the
Macintosh twins. I wrote down every word.

10.02 a.m.
Suspect 3:
Name not known yet.

"A thousand greetings!
I'm Ali Guffaw, Genie to his
Majesty, the Sultan of Azmir."

Oh, sure!
We detectives hear
a lot of weird
stories—but this
was just too weird.
Mrs Hartley was
going to go mad
when she heard
about this.

The twins helped the
man called Ali to his
feet. His bones
creaked, and he
moaned and
groaned. Finally,
he stood up straight
and looked around.

That was when the
trouble really started.

Chapter 3

Ali Makes Things Worse

This was a great detective job. I would probably get a prize. Just then, Ali started to say he would get the twins out of trouble.

Not with me, Denny Davidson, Detective on the job, he wouldn't!

Ali folded his arms and cast a spell. I was sure *that* was against the museum's rules!

Suddenly, every jar in the museum started twisting and turning.

One by one, they toppled and tumbled to the floor.

I watched in horror as all of the ancient jars smashed into pieces. Those Macintosh twins had gone too far!

I was ready to jump out and surprise them all, when Maude and Mickey started to speak.

10.04 a.m.
Suspect 1 and Suspect 2:

"Oh, no! Let's get out of here!"

Before I could leap out from my hiding place and call Mrs Hartley, the suspects ran through the exit door. All three of them escaped.
I had to do what any good detective would do.
I had to follow them.

As I ran out onto the museum steps, I realised I should write a description of Ali, in case he got away.

10.05 a.m.
Suspect 3:
Ali Guffaw.

Description:
Wearing baggy trousers, pointy shoes and a colourful jacket. Obviously a disguise so no-one knows who he really is.

But he was clever, that Ali Guffaw. People were stopping and staring at him. He must have realised that his disguise was not working.

What did he do? He folded his arms and cast another spell.

In an instant, everyone in the street was wearing the same clothes as Ali. The Macintosh twins were not going to get away with this!

Even I was wearing the same weird clothes!
This detective job was becoming *very* strange.

Chapter 4
A Flying Carpet

Next, I hid behind a
rubbish tin close by.
I wrote down what I saw
happen next.

Ali's next spell made a
colourful carpet appear.

"Let's go!" he smiled at
the twins, pointing at
the carpet.

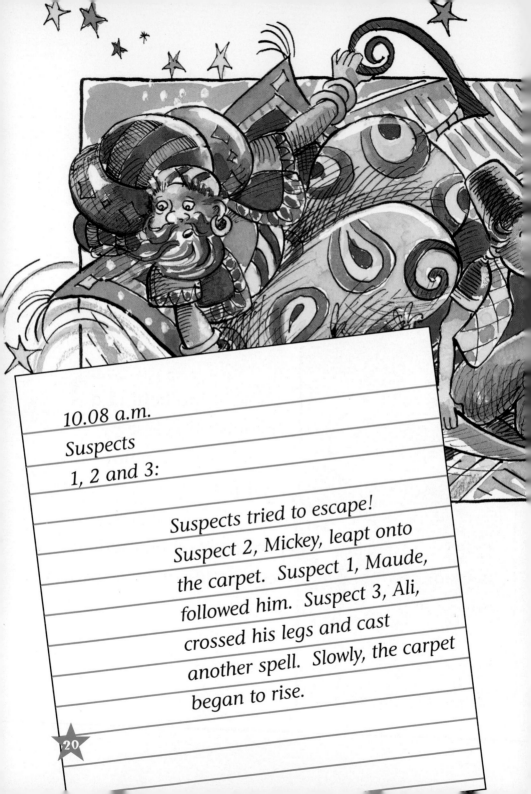

10.08 a.m.

Suspects

1, 2 and 3:

Suspects tried to escape!
Suspect 2, Mickey, leapt onto
the carpet. Suspect 1, Maude,
followed him. Suspect 3, Ali,
crossed his legs and cast
another spell. Slowly, the carpet
began to rise.

The flying carpet dangled dangerously above the street. Mrs Hartley would be really angry when she heard my report. Breaking jars, running away from school trips, and riding on flying carpets.

The twins would have extra homework for weeks! I couldn't help grinning!

As if flying on a carpet wasn't bad enough, they then started to do dangerous tricks on it. They tipped to the left. They tipped to the right. They started spinning around.

Then, someone yelled at them. When I turned to see who it was, there was an old man standing there.

10.10 a.m.

Suspect 4:

Name not known yet.

"ALI GUFFAW!" said Suspect 4.

"Come down here now!"

Suspect 3 and 4 know each

other.

I suspect they are probably

in a gang!

My suspicions were right. Ali brought the carpet down, and hugged the old man.

They had probably done all sorts of crimes together, I thought.

Then, all four suspects tried to escape again. They went around a corner. I followed behind them, trying not to get spotted. But there was no chance of that. They were all too busy planning and plotting their next terrible crime!

Chapter 5

The Hide-Out

As I followed them around another corner, I found myself in a part of town that I did not know. They walked around another corner.

Finally, they stopped in front of an old shop. A sign said that it was called 'The Sultan of Azmir's Restaurant.'

This was probably the hide-out for the gang.
I looked around for a street name or a street
number. But they had been too clever.
I couldn't find out where I was!

Just as I was about to try and find my way back
to the museum to tell Mrs Hartley all about my
detective work, something amazing happened.

Ali folded his arms and cast his final spell.
In a flash, the Macintosh twins disappeared!

Normally, if anyone had made the Macintosh
twins disappear, I would have been glad!
But this was *very* suspicious.

Chapter **6**

A Detective In Trouble

I raced back down the street, and turned the corner. I had to get help, fast!

I turned left, then right. But I was lost. It took me hours to get back to the museum.

That's when my plan started to go wrong. I was
amazed to see my whole class waiting on the
museum steps. And those Macintosh twins were
there, too, looking as if nothing had happened.

But worse still, Mrs Hartley was there. And
she did not look very happy.

She was looking at her watch and had a very
angry look on her face.

"Denny Davidson!" she said in a loud voice.

Mrs Hartley pointed her finger at me, and the rest of the class giggled.

"Where have you been?" she asked

I realised that I was still wearing the same strange clothes as Ali Guffaw. Somehow those sneaky Macintosh twins had changed their clothes back to normal!

I started to explain, but Mrs Hartley was not in the mood to listen.

"You have been out running around while you should have been in the museum doing school work," she said, frowning at me.

"But, Mrs Hartley," I started to explain.

"And, what's worse, you are late! We've been waiting for hours! You are in *very big trouble*, Denny Davidson."

So that's my story. Instead of those Macintosh twins getting into trouble, I'm the one who has weeks of extra homework. It's just not fair.